The Thing That Ate Aunt Julia

Nicholas Allan

Dial Books for Young Readers NEW YORK

For Nicholas Bremer

First published in the United States 1991 by
Dial Books for Young Readers
A Division of Penguin Books USA Inc.
375 Hudson Street
New York, New York 10014

Published in Great Britain by Hutchinson Children's Books
An imprint of Century Hutchinson Ltd.
Copyright © 1990 by Nicholas Allan

Library of Congress Cataloging in Publication Data
Allan, Nicholas. The thing that ate Aunt Julia.
Summary: When super-neat Aunt Julia throws
Jeffrey's magic potion down the toilet,
the toilet, much to Jeffrey's delight, comes
alive and terrorizes the neighborhood.
[1. Aunts—Fiction. 2. Magic—Fiction.
3. Humorous stories] I. Title.
PZ7.A412Th 1991   [E]   89-71535
ISBN 0-8037-0872-6

Jeffrey lived with his strict Aunt Julia. She had rules about tidiness.

Jeffrey wasn't even allowed to play with toys, or friends,
in case he damaged the furniture or broke something.

One day he opened up his great-great-grandfather's cabinet. His great-great-grandfather had been an inventor.

Inside, Jeffrey found a bottle of Thick Yellow Goo, and on the label it said "100% PURE MAGIC USE WITH CARE."

Jeffrey poured the Goo into some cups and spoons. This is what happened:

Suddenly Aunt Julia came in.

She was so angry she snatched the bottle and poured all the Goo down the toilet.

Then she sent Jeffrey straight to bed.

That night Jeffrey thought about the Thick Yellow Goo. Early the next morning he was still thinking about it when, from the bathroom, he heard some noises—some gurgling, spluttering, bubbling noises.

Something strange was going on in there. . . .

And it got stranger . . .

and stranger.

Jeffrey crept
out of bed just in
time to see
something slink
out of the
bathroom.

At first Jeffrey
was afraid, but
the "something"
looked friendly.

It also looked hungry.

Jeffrey gave it some bread. But it didn't like that, so he gave it some of Aunt Julia's plates, which it did like —*very* much.

It ate the forks and the kitchen table, then wandered around the house chomping and chewing. A nibble here, a nibble there.

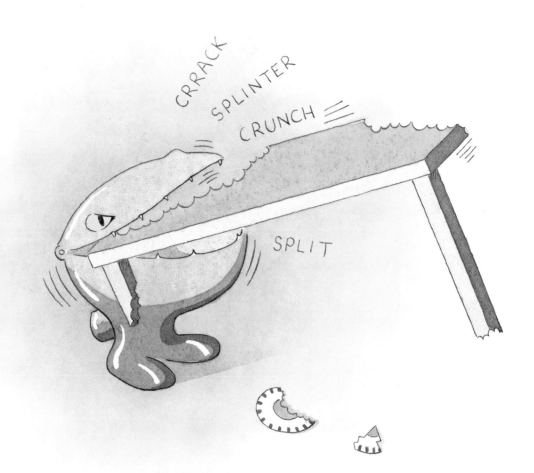

It ate:

a vase,

a piano,

a lampshade,

a picture,

a Persian carpet,

a brooch,

a chest of drawers,

a sofa,

two armchairs,

a Louis XIV
carriage clock,

a washing machine,

a hair dryer,

a dishwasher,

a potted plant,

a color television,

and . . .

an aunt.

When the house was empty they did a little dance.
Jeffrey was *so* pleased with his new friend.

They chased each other . . .

and played basketball . . .

and hide-and-seek.

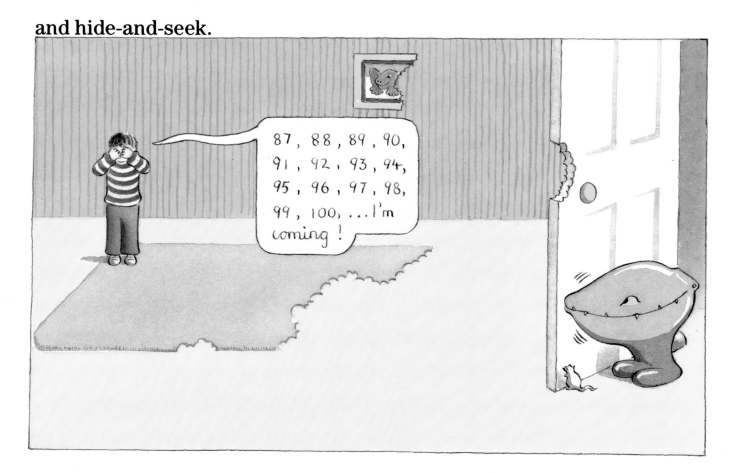

87, 88, 89, 90, 91, 92, 93, 94, 95, 96, 97, 98, 99, 100, . . . I'm coming!

After that they went out and scared people . . .

which was *a lot* of fun.

Finally they went to a railroad station and caught a train.
They had a wonderful ride all the way to the beach.

Jeffrey's friend loved water and flushed with excitement
when it saw the ocean. They went for a quick swim together.

TOILETS
THIS WAY →

Afterward they lay in the sun to dry. Jeffrey bought an ice cream and gave his friend the wrapper to eat. Then he told some very silly jokes, which made the thing gurgle and splutter with watery laughter.

Toward the end of the afternoon they walked back to the station and caught the train. It had been a day to remember.

When they arrived home, Jeffrey's friend began to feel tired. Jeffrey realized the Yellow Goo was running out.

Very slowly the thing started to change back into its old self. Jeffrey was sad. Suddenly he felt very alone. But just then an amazing thing happened. Its mouth began to open.

And out stepped . . . Aunt Julia!

She seemed none the worse for wear. In fact she was so happy to be back and to see Jeffrey again, she didn't care about the house anymore—not even the Louis XIV carriage clock.

From then on Jeffrey and Aunt Julia lived happily together. Jeffrey was allowed to play wherever he liked. And the toilet stayed put in the bathroom, right where it belonged.

THE END